DEDICATION
This book is dedicated to my son Connor Newman.
There is nothing more special than the joy seen in the eyes
of a young child as they experience their first bird.

Published by Struik Nature
(an imprint of Penguin Random House South Africa (Pty) Ltd)
The Estuaries No. 4, Oxbow Crescent,
Century Avenue, Century City, 7441
PO Box 1144, Cape Town, 8000 South Africa

Reg. No. 1953/000441/07

Visit www.penguinrandomhouse.co.za and join the Struik Nature Club
for updates, news, events, and special offers

First published in 2008
9 10 8

Copyright © in text, 2008: Doug Newman

Copyright © in maps, 2008: Penguin Random House South Africa (Pty) Ltd

Copyright © in photographs, 2008: Doug Newman,
with the exception of the following: Shaen Adey: page 7 (right); Sam J Basch: front cover top centre right;
page 29 (right); Tony Camacho: page 19 (left); Nigel J Dennis: back cover bottom (both); back cover top centre
left; front cover bottom (all), pages 7 (left), 8 (right), 10 (both), 11 (left), 12, 13 (left), 16 (left), 17 (both), 21 (right),
22 (right), 23 (left), 31 (right), 32 (right); Albert Froneman: front cover top right; pages 18 (both), 22 (left),
23 (right), 24 (left), 26 (left), 27 (both), 30 (both), 36 (right), 38 (right); Peter Pickford: front cover top centre left;
page 19 (right), 24 (right), 33 (left), 37 (right); Chris Rawlings: contents page; Peter Ryan: front cover deep etch (left);
page 20 (right); Mark Skinner: page 35 (right); Warwick Tarboton: pages 20 (left), 21 (left);
Ariadne van Zandbergen: front cover top left; page 26 (right), 32 (left); Maggie Westrop: page 38 (left)

Copyright © in bird call recordings, 2008: Doug Newman, with the exception of
the Southern Ground Hornbill and Common Ostrich, copyright © The Transvaal Museum

Copyright © in published edition, 2008: Penguin Random House South Africa (Pty) Ltd

Publishing manager: Pippa Parker
Editor: Helen de Villiers
Proofreader: Emily Bowles
Design director: Janice Evans
Designer: Martin Endemann

Reproduction by Hirt & Carter Cape (Pty) Ltd
Printed and bound in China by Leo Paper Products Ltd.

Penguin Random House is committed to a sustainable future for
our business, our readers and our planet. This book is made from
Forest Stewardship Council® certified paper.

All rights reserved. No part of this publication may be reproduced, stored in
a retrieval system, or transmitted, in any form or by any means, electronic,
mechanical, photocopying, recording or otherwise, without the prior
written permission of the copyright holder(s).

ISBN: 978 1 77007 678 5

CONTENTS

Introduction to bird sounds	4
How to use this book	5
Learning about birds from their calls	6
60 birds featured in full colour with simple text and maps	7
References	39
Index	40

INSIDE BACK COVER -
CD WITH 60 BIRD CALLS

INTRODUCTION TO BIRD SOUNDS

Bird sounds – of one sort or another – are everywhere. These sounds can vary greatly: thrushes sing beautiful songs, woodpeckers drum on tree trunks, and some birds click wing feathers together or make snapping sounds with their beaks. This book and CD deal mainly with bird calls.

Most birds sing at dawn as soon as the sun rises; this is called the 'dawn chorus'. If you have never heard it, get up early and go out into your garden. Listen to how many different types of bird are calling at once and just how wonderful the sound is. Birds call early because sound travels best in the cool morning air, and this means many more neighbours will hear their song.

There are as many different bird calls as there are different types of bird. Some birds have a beautiful song, like the Olive Thrush or the Black-throated Canary. Others have harsh, unmusical voices, such as the Pied Crow or the White-breasted Cormorant.

Birds use their calls for many different reasons, but most often to protect their territory or to find a mate.

Rufous-naped Larks, for instance, call from the tops of bushes or from fence posts. They do this either to tell others that the territory is taken, or to tell mates that they have a territory and are ready to raise chicks. Watch how Common Mynas chatter as they fight over your garden, each laying claim to the territory for raising their young.

The Cape Bunting's call is a piercing 'dzeeu-dzeeu-tree-it-tree-dzeeu-dzeeu-tree-dzeeu-treu-treu'.

HOW TO USE THIS BOOK

- This book, together with the CD, will teach you to recognise some of the amazing sounds our birds make. The book features a photograph and some information on each of the 60 birds. It tells you where to find them, if they are here all year or if they are only visiting us, and what they eat. A map next to each bird shows in which regions you can look for them.

- On the CD you are given a little information about each bird before you hear its call. Use the CD with the book to match the pictures of the birds with the sounds they make.
- As you learn and remember the sounds, you will be able to look for those birds when you hear them. Simply follow the call and look for the bird that's making it.

CD track number and common name of bird.

The distribution map shows the parts of southern Africa in which the bird can be seen.

Look out for the icons that indicate food and nesting information.

Information about the call and the corresponding track number can be found at the bottom of the pages.

13 | Crowned Lapwing
Kroonkiewiet

Crowned Lapwings are common birds found across most of southern Africa, but only in areas with short grass, such as at airports or on sports fields.

These birds do not migrate, and often live in the same area all year round. When the grass turns dull and brown in winter, the lapwings' movement and striking black, brown and white colouring make the dull winter grass come to life.

 Insects and termites are their favourite food items.

 Their nest is a scrape in the ground in open areas. Even though the nest is not covered, it is well disguised and is very difficult to spot.

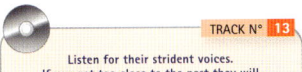

TRACK N° 13

Listen for their strident voices. If you get too close to the nest they will even dive-bomb you to chase you away.

14 | Spotted Thick-knee
Gewone Dikkop

Spotted Thick-knees are widespread across most of southern Africa.

They are found in open areas covered with short grass, such as at airports and sports fields or on land that has been well grazed, as well as on stony ground.

These birds are resident all year round. They rest during the day, but if you look carefully at the edges of sports fields, you may see them resting in the shade under a bush. They are active in the evening, and particularly noisy during the breeding season.

 They eat spiders and many kinds of insect, including termites and locusts.

 They lay their eggs on the ground, usually without even a scrape being made, and the nest is not always well hidden.

TRACK N° 14

During the day they are silent, but their ghostly whistles at sunset and at night make this bird easy to identify.

LEARNING ABOUT BIRDS FROM THEIR CALLS

Different birds have different calls. What's more, if you watch and listen closely, you will notice that the same bird makes a range of sounds. Each call serves a different purpose.

Young Karoo Thrushes, for example, have various calls: one to tell their parents where they are, and another to call for food. The first call will encourage their parents to stay close by; the second will make the parents set off to fetch food for their young. Most birds have an alarm call to tell others that danger is near and that they should leave the area. 'Display' calls tell females that the male is looking for a mate.

Listening to bird calls is a good way of finding out what birds are up to, which opens up for us the amazing world of bird behaviour. After hearing a particular call, we can even start to predict what a bird will do next. Pick a bird in your garden and watch it closely. Write down each of its calls – as they sound to you – in a book, as well as what the bird was doing when it made that sound. Soon you will start to understand the reasons for their sounds – in other words, to understand their language. You will be well on your way to becoming a bird scientist!

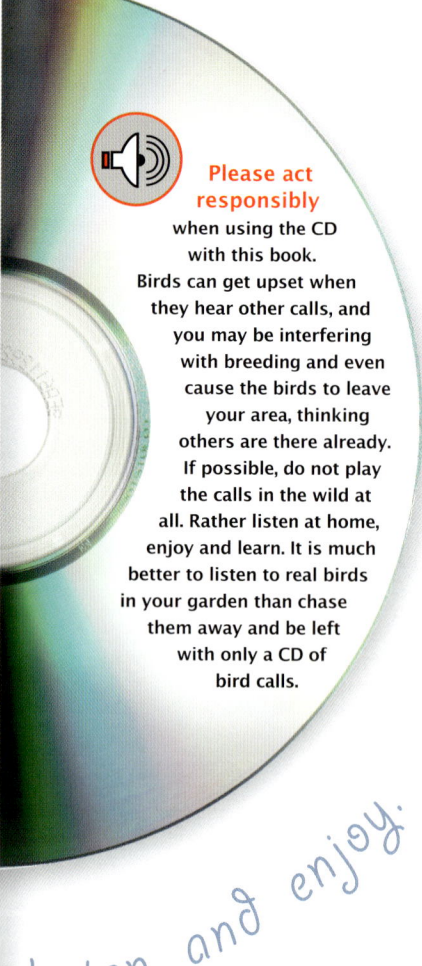

Please act responsibly when using the CD with this book. Birds can get upset when they hear other calls, and you may be interfering with breeding and even cause the birds to leave your area, thinking others are there already. If possible, do not play the calls in the wild at all. Rather listen at home, enjoy and learn. It is much better to listen to real birds in your garden than chase them away and be left with only a CD of bird calls.

Most importantly, listen and enjoy.

1 | African Penguin
Brilpikkewyn

Seen on Boulders Beach, adult African Penguins (left); juvenile (right).

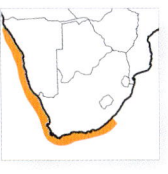

African Penguins are endangered birds that live along some of our coasts and on a few small offshore islands, including Robben Island – and nowhere else in the world.

Penguins cannot fly; their wings serve as hard flippers at sea, so that they can swim almost as fast as sharks. Their feathers have adapted to act as waterproofing and insulation against the cold. They spend most of their time at sea looking for food, but come on to land to nest and breed at a few rocky beaches, such as Boulders Beach in Simonstown. They must also remain on land once a season to lose their old feathers and grow new ones – this takes about three weeks.

African Penguins do not migrate, but stay in southern African waters all year round.

 These birds eat mainly fish. However, over-fishing by humans has reduced fish supplies, meaning that penguins have less to eat. Dwindling food supplies is one of the reasons that the African Penguin is an endangered bird.

 They make their nests by digging a tunnel into the ground. On some islands conservation authorities have built artificial 'penguin houses' to encourage them to breed. Penguins nesting on beaches use dense bushes or rocky overhangs as nest shelters. They usually lay two eggs, which the male and female take equal turns sitting on. While one sits on the nest, the other heads off to sea to feed.

TRACK N° 01

Their call sounds much like that of a donkey, which is why these birds used to be called Jackass Penguins.

2 | Little Grebe
Kleindobbertjie

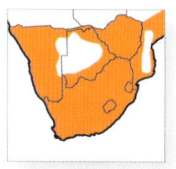

Little Grebes are tiny waterbirds, commonly found all over southern Africa. You can spot them at almost any freshwater pan or wetland, often chasing each other across the water to defend their territory.

They usually stay in the same place all year, moving only if the water level drops too low, or if it becomes necessary to search for food elsewhere.

 Watch them as they dive under the water. They disappear for quite a while, as they search for insects, small fish, tadpoles and frogs.

 The nest is made of plants, and floats on the water; it is tied to some stable object in the water to stop it from floating away.

TRACK N° 02

Their call is quite distinctive – it sounds a lot like a high-pitched giggle.

3 | White-breasted Cormorant
Witborsduiker

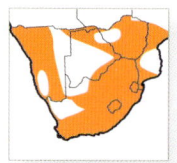

White-breasted Cormorants are found across most of southern Africa.

They can be seen on rivers, freshwater ponds and dams and even along the coast.

As resident birds, they stay here all year round and only travel to find food, or in search of suitable colonies in which to build their nests.

 They hunt for fish by diving underwater, and capture their prey with their large, hooked beaks.

 These cormorants make their nest on power-line pylons or dead trees close to water. They build a very large nest of sticks and anything else that helps support the nest or hold it together.

TRACK N° 03

Their call is a harsh, rasping sound, a bit like someone laughing, and can be heard most often at breeding sites.

4 | Hadeda Ibis
Hadeda

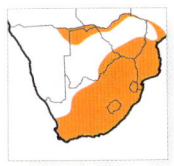

Hadedas are very common birds across most of South Africa, except for in the very dry areas.

They can be found almost anywhere that has some trees, but particularly near wetlands and rivers, and often in gardens.

They do not migrate, and so can be seen all year round.

 Most of their diet consists of insects, which they dig out of the ground with their long, curved beaks. They also eat crickets, and in Gauteng they even eat 'Parktown prawns'.

 They make their nest, a small platform of branches and twigs, in big trees.

TRACK N° 04

They call as they fly overhead, singing 'Ha-ha-hadeda' – which shows where their name comes from.

5 | Egyptian Goose
Kolgans

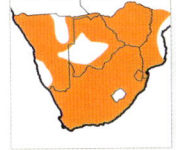

Wherever you find water in southern Africa, you will find Egyptian Geese.

Look for them around rivers, dams, wetlands and almost any stretch of fresh water. However, because they do not like salt water, you will not see them near the beach.

They stay in one place all year round and can be spotted in their range whether it's summer or winter.

 Water plants are their favourite food, but they will also eat grass seeds. You can sometimes spot them eating greenery or seeds in farm fields.

 Their nest is made in many different sorts of places, mostly on the ground, but sometimes in trees or on cliffs.

TRACK N° 05

They call like any other goose, making hisses and other harsh sounds.

6 | Yellow-billed Duck
Geelbekeend

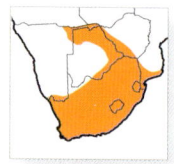

Yellow-billed Ducks are very common waterbirds found all over South Africa.

You can see them at almost all inland water-bodies, such as dams or wetlands, but they do not like fast-flowing rivers.

These birds do not migrate, and remain in the same areas all year round.

 They mostly eat small water plants, but also insects that live in the water.

 They build their nest on the ground near water. A shallow bowl, it is lined thickly with grass and duck down to make it cosy. These ducks hide their nests so well in the thick grass, and often under a thorny bush, that you will not easily be able to find one.

TRACK N° 06

They quack like all ducks, and also make other duck-like sounds.

7 | African Fish-Eagle
Visarend

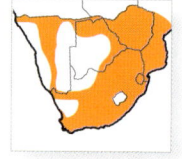

These eagles are found in most of the eastern and southern parts of South Africa, and particularly in the Western Cape.

You will spot them at most large areas of water, such as big rivers and dams.

They can often be seen flying overhead or perched high up overlooking the water, on the watch for food.

They remain in a particular area all year, and only move when the waterbody totally dries up.

 Their main diet is fish. Watch them as they swoop down over the water to catch a tasty victim.

 They build a large stick nest on top of a tree, sometimes in a dead tree.

TRACK N° 07

Their call is well known: some people call it the 'sound of Africa', and you can hear it sometimes in movies and wildlife programmes set in Africa.

8 | Jackal Buzzard
Rooiborsjakkalsvoël

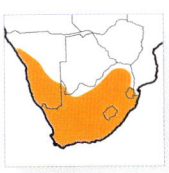

Jackal Buzzards are fairly common birds of prey, found mainly in South Africa. They are most common in the Western Cape, but they also occur across the rest of the country, except the very dry parts of the Northern Cape.

They like hilly areas, and are found wherever hills meet fynbos, grassland, or semi-desert and even in hilly woodland areas.

Although they do not migrate, they travel about looking for food.

 Like most birds of prey, they catch many different creatures, from birds and small mammals to reptiles and frogs. They drop down very fast out of the air to seize their prey with their talons.

 Their nest is a large platform of sticks lined with soft feathers and leaves.

 TRACK N° 08

As the birds' name suggests, their call sounds like that of a jackal, a common animal of the African bushveld.

9 | Swainson's Spurfowl
Bosveldfisant

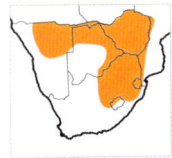

Swainson's Spurfowl are common in the Free State, Gauteng, Limpopo and Mpumalanga, as well as in our neighbouring countries.

Spurfowl and their similar-looking cousins, the francolins, are generally difficult to see because they live in grasslands where they are well hidden, but you can sometimes spot them feeding in the open.

All spurfowl are resident birds and can be found in the same place right through the year.

 Their diet includes many different types of plant matter, such as berries, bulbs and leaves.

 Their nest is just a scrape in the ground in dense grass or bushes, where it is hard to find.

 TRACK N° 09

Their harsh, croaking call can be heard early in the morning, telling others that the territory is occupied.

Male Common Ostriches are black and females are grey.

10 | Common Ostrich
Volstruis

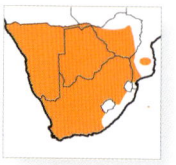

Ostriches are found all over southern Africa, but are not common in the wild and can be seen mainly in protected areas and on farms.

They live anywhere from semi-desert areas to bushveld and woodland.

Because these huge birds (they are the largest living birds in the world) cannot fly, they do not travel very far from their particular area. However, they can run faster than any other bird, at speeds of up to 65 kilometres per hour. You can often see them on farms, where they are kept for their feathers, skin and meat.

Ostriches will either hide when they are threatened, by lying flat on the ground, or they will run away. But if cornered, they can kick very viciously and have been known to cause terrible injury with their claws, and even death.

Ostriches eat mainly grasses, roots and the leaves of trees, but they will also eat insects. They swallow small stones and other hard objects, which they do not digest, but which help break up the food they eat.

Their nest is a simple scrape in the ground in sandy areas. Their massive eggs (the largest of any bird) can weigh up to one-and-a-half kilograms each. Several females lay their eggs in a single, communal nest, which may contain up to 60 eggs. For camouflage, the dusty grey female sits on the eggs during the day, keeping them at a constant temperature, and the black male sits on them at night.

TRACK N° 10

Their call is a deep, booming 'oooom-ooom-oooooooommmmm'.

11 | Helmeted Guineafowl
Gewone Tarentaal

12 | Red-knobbed Coot
Bleshoender

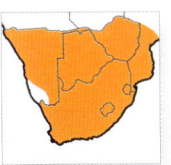 Helmeted Guineafowl are the most common grassland game birds of southern Africa.

They can be found from bushveld to the edges of forests – even in the dry Karoo.

They are year-round residents, and you can see them feeding in the open in grassland and on farms.

 Their diet includes anything from harvested grain to insects and roots. They help to control many insects that are pests to farmers.

 Their nests are often no more than a scrape in the ground in thick grass or under a bush, usually near open areas that are good for feeding.

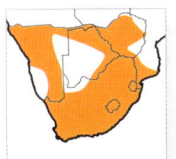 Red-knobbed Coots can be found wherever there is open water across most of southern Africa.

They like water that is still, and where they can find water plants to feed on. Look for them on dams, pans and wetlands.

They do not migrate, and will often remain in just one area, only moving to a new neighbourhood if the water level drops too low or there is not enough food.

 They eat many different types of food, from algae to grass, and even small insects that live in the water.

 Their nest is a large, floating platform of reeds.

TRACK N° 11
Their whistling call, and particularly the gurgling calls of the males, make it easy to find these birds.

TRACK N° 12
They make many different sounds, from short, abrupt noises to rasping, deep sounds. Listen carefully and you should easily find these birds in just about any wetland.

13 | Crowned Lapwing
Kroonkiewiet

Crowned Lapwings are common birds found across most of southern Africa, but only in areas with short grass, such as at airports or on sports fields.

These birds do not migrate, and often live in the same area all year round. When the grass turns dull and brown in winter, the lapwings' movement and striking black, brown and white colouring make the dull winter grass come to life.

 Insects and termites are their favourite food items.

 Their nest is a scrape in the ground in open areas. Even though the nest is not covered, it is well disguised and is very difficult to spot.

 TRACK N° 13

Listen for their strident voices.
If you get too close to the nest they will even dive-bomb you to chase you away.

14 | Spotted Thick-knee
Gewone Dikkop

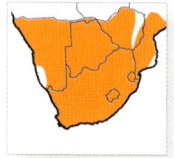

Spotted Thick-knees are widespread across most of southern Africa.

They are found in open areas covered with short grass, such as at airports and sports fields or on land that has been well grazed, as well as on stony ground.

These birds are resident all year round. They rest during the day, but if you look carefully at the edges of sports fields, you may see them resting in the shade under a bush. They are active in the evening, and particularly noisy during the breeding season.

 They eat spiders and many kinds of insect, including termites and locusts.

 They lay their eggs on the ground, usually without even making a scrape; the nest is not always well hidden.

 TRACK N° 14

During the day they are silent, but their ghostly whistles at sunset and at night make this bird easy to identify.

15 | Kelp Gull
Kelpmeeu

These are the most common of the large sea gulls along our coastline, all the way from KwaZulu-Natal into Namibia.

Kelp Gulls can be found anywhere from coastal rubbish dumps to off-shore, where they fly out to sea in search of food.

These gulls are resident in southern Africa all year round, although they travel along the coasts on the lookout for food.

 As scavengers, they look for old shellfish and any other fish scraps. They can be seen hovering around fishing boats, waiting for scraps, and around rubbish dumps, looking for tasty treats.

 Their nest ranges from a simple scrape to a rough bowl made of seaweed, kelp, feathers and other beach debris.

TRACK N° 15

Their call is that of typical sea gulls. Go to almost any beach-front area and you will hear them.

16 | Grey-headed Gull
Gryskopmeeu

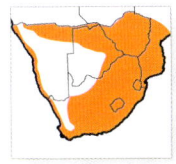

Grey-headed Gulls are not widespread, but where they do occur, they are very common and gather in large numbers. They live along most of our coastline, although in the Western Cape you are more likely to find Hartlaub's Gull at the beach. Grey-headed Gulls also visit inland dams, pans and wetlands in the Free State and Gauteng.

Although these gulls do not migrate, they do move around when food supplies run low.

 They look for small aquatic insects and fish, swooping down to catch them. They also scavenge and can often be seen at rubbish dumps.

 They make a shallow, bowl-shaped grass nest near water. They may also take over old nests, such as those of Red-knobbed Coots.

TRACK N° 16

Their call is typical of a gull, although it is not as loud or as harsh as that of the Kelp Gull.

17 | Cape Turtle-Dove
Gewone Tortelduif

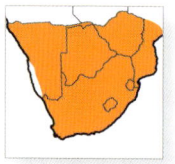

Cape Turtle-Doves are very common in southern Africa, and are often seen in gardens.
They live in areas with lots of trees; you may even find them in plantations of exotic trees.

These birds do not migrate, and stay in one area all year round. They call throughout the year, so you will probably hear them even in winter.

 Although they eat insects, most of their food consists of seed of various types. They are often seen at garden bird feeders, looking for seed that has fallen on the ground.

 They make a small nest of twigs and leaves, but are also known to take over the nests of other birds.

 TRACK N° 17

Their call, typically dove-like, is a 'ko-kuuuurrr-ur', repeated over and over again.

18 | Laughing Dove
Rooiborsduifie

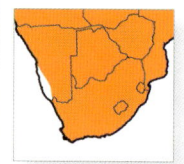

Laughing Doves are the most common doves in southern Africa – you can find them just about anywhere.
They inhabit most areas where there are trees, and are common in almost all gardens.

As non-migratory birds, they can be found at any time of the year, and mostly don't move from their habitual area.

 Like most doves, their food is made up of seeds but they may also eat roots. Put out seed at your garden bird feeder, and they should visit your garden very soon.

 Their nest is small and made of twigs and roots, but they are also known to use the old nests of other birds.

 TRACK N° 18

Their call is like a soft, bubbling laugh. This is why they are called Laughing Doves.

19 | Grey Go-away-bird
Kwêvoël

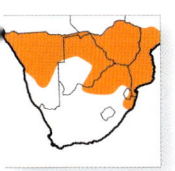

Grey Go-away-birds are found in Gauteng, Limpopo, Mpumalanga and in neighbouring countries.
They are bushveld birds and are also found in gardens and woodlands. Their distinctive call will help you find them easily.

Go-away-birds stay here all year round and never travel very far within their range.

 Fruit is their favourite food but they can also eat parts of flowers and plants. They may even eat some insects.

 Their flimsy-looking nest is an unlined platform of dry twigs, most often built in a thorn tree.

TRACK N° 19

These birds are best known for their call – it is where they get the name Go-away-bird. It sounds as if they are calling go-away to warn other animals of danger from hunters or predators.

20 | Diderick Cuckoo
Diederikkie

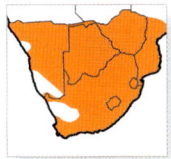

These cuckoos are common summer visitors to most of southern Africa, except the Karoo and desert areas.
They enjoy many types of habitat, but prefer woodlands and bushveld. They call from the tops of tall trees, making them fairly easy to find. They can often be spotted in the open, sitting on a fence.

As summer visitors, they migrate north during our winter. They can be seen locally from October to February.

 Their main diet is caterpillars, but they are known also to eat the eggs inside nests they take over.

 Like all southern African cuckoos, they always lay their eggs in other birds' nests, leaving the new hosts to raise their young.

TRACK N° 20

Their call is easy to learn, and gives the bird its name: it sounds like 'di-di-di-diderick'.

21 | Red-chested Cuckoo
Piet-my-vrou

Adult Red-chested Cuckoo (left); juvenile (right,

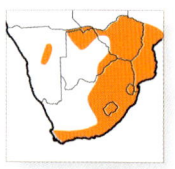

Red-chested Cuckoos are common summer visitors to the eastern and central parts of southern Africa. They also visit along the coast as far south as Cape Town, but not the drier western parts of the country.

Forests and dense woodland are the places to look for them, but they may also be found in gardens with large trees. Because they are shy and move about singly, they are difficult to spot; but they are very vocal and you will often hear them calling.

Almost all cuckoos are migrants, and the Red-chested Cuckoo leaves southern Africa during our winter. The time to see them is in summer – from October to April.

 Most of their diet consists of insects, but they may also eat berries, and sometimes even other birds' eggs.

 They do not build their own nest, but instead lay their eggs – up to 20 per season – in other birds' nests, removing an egg from each nest in which they lay. Some of the host birds are robins, thrushes, wagtails and flycatchers. The cuckoos leave their eggs to hatch in these host nests and the chicks to be raised by the owners of the nests. The hosts don't seem to realise that they are hatching and raising other birds' babies. The cuckoo eggs usually hatch first, and the baby birds kick the host birds' eggs out of the nest. Adult Red-chested Cuckoos never see their young while they are growing up.

TRACK N° 21

Their call is unique and gives the Red-chested Cuckoo its Afrikaans name: it calls 'piet-my-vrou'.

22 | Burchell's Coucal
Gewone Vleiloerie

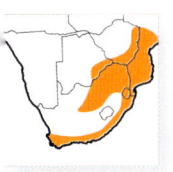

These are fairly common birds, found in Limpopo, Mpumalanga, parts of Gauteng and along the coast down to Cape Town.

They are very secretive and stay hidden in thick vegetation. They live in forests, dense woodlands and on the edges of wetlands. If your garden has overgrown areas, you may even find them there.

Burchell's Coucals like to stay in one place and they never travel too far away.

 As predatory birds, they eat mice and young nestlings. You may even see them eating reptiles, insects and small snakes.

 They build their deep nest of grass and leaves in reed beds or other thick vegetation.

TRACK N° 22

It's believed that when they call they are telling us that rain is coming. Listen for the deep bubbling 'du-du-du...' call.

23 | Spotted Eagle-Owl
Gevlekte Ooruil

These are fairly common owls that are found in most of southern Africa.

They are nocturnal, so you can find them out and about at night. They live in various habitats, from cities to woodlands, on forest edges and in mountainous areas.

Because they do not migrate and are territorial, you will find them always within the same small area.

 Like other owls, they eat many kinds of prey, such as rodents up to the size of rabbits, other birds, such as francolins, and snakes.

 They nest in widely varying places, from a ledge on a cliff to a scrape in the ground. They have even been known to nest in window boxes on houses.

TRACK N° 23

Their call, a conversation between two birds, is a very soft, owl-like hooting – 'hoo-hoo-hooooooo'. The male gives a two-note 'hoo-hoo' and the female replies with a three-note 'hoo-hoo-hooooooo'.

24 | Pearl-spotted Owlet
Witkoluil

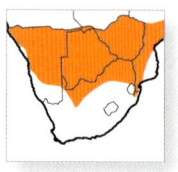

Pearl-spotted Owlets are common bushveld birds found in northern Gauteng, Limpopo, Mpumalanga and further north in Namibia, Botswana and Zimbabwe.

They prefer woodland and bushveld, but their favourite habitat is thornveld.

Non-migrant, year-round residents, they stay in a localised area. Although they are mainly active at night, you can nevertheless sometimes see them moving around during the day.

 Like other small owls, they catch mainly insects, but also vertebrates such as mice, and even other small birds.

 They make their nest in trees where they use natural holes (they cannot make their own holes), and may also take over old, unused nests.

 TRACK N° 24

Listen out for their piercing whistle call. You will hear it almost every night in bushveld areas.

25 | Little Swift
Kleinwindswael

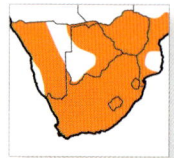

These are among the most common of the swifts in southern Africa.

They are fairly easy to spot as they fly around, feeding in the air near their nests.

Most Little Swifts leave southern Africa to winter elsewhere, but little is known about where they go, and in some areas they stay all year round.

 Little Swifts eat only insects, which they catch in the air. They move around looking for areas with lots of insects, and gathering in as many as possible whenever there's a plentiful supply.

 They make their nest using bits and pieces collected in flight, like loose strands of grass, and bind it together with saliva. Their nests are located high up, on buildings or cliffs.

 TRACK N° 25

Their call makes them easy to find: listen out for the high-pitched, twittering trill.

26 | Red-faced Mousebird
Rooiwangmuisvoël

These are the most widely spread of the mousebirds. You can find them almost everywhere in southern Africa, except in deserts and other dry areas.

Groups of trees in grassy bushveld areas are the best places to look for them, as well as along rivers. You might even find them in your garden.

Because they do not migrate, they can be found all year round, although they might move to a new area if there is a shortage of food.

 Their diet consists mainly of fruit, but they sometimes eat flowers too.

 These mousebirds make a small, cup-shaped nest of twigs lined with soft material.

TRACK N° 26

Their call is easy to recognise – a soft, whistled three-note call – 'chee-ree-ree'.

27 | Pied Kingfisher
Bontvisvanger

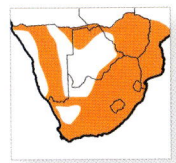

Pied Kingfishers occur in most of the eastern and central parts of southern Africa, and along the coast down to Cape Town.

They can be found wherever there is fresh water with food. Farm dams, rivers, wetlands and lakes are all places to watch for this elegant-looking kingfisher.

These birds are resident and remain in their particular area all year round, but may move away if water levels in the area drop.

 Their diet includes small fish and insects. They catch fish by hovering over the water and then diving suddenly to grab prey.

 To make their nest, they burrow into a sand bank; the entrance tunnel to the nest can be over a metre long.

TRACK N° 27

Their call is a high-pitched series of twittering noises.

28 | European Bee-eater
Europese Byvreter

29 | Lilac-breasted Roller
Gewone Troupant

These summer visitors can be found across most of southern Africa, except in parts of the Free State and KwaZulu-Natal.

They live in a wide range of habitats and can be found almost anywhere that offers places on which to perch.

Absent from our part of the world in winter, these migrant birds can be spotted locally from October through to May.

 Their diet consists entirely of insects, which they catch in the air while flying.

 Their nest is a tunnel, which they make in a sand bank – often a man-made bank – and they usually nest in colonies of up to 30 pairs of birds.

TRACK N° 28

Listen out for the bubbly-sounding 'puurrrp' they make. You will often hear this, and variations on the call, as a flock of them flies overhead on the hunt for food.

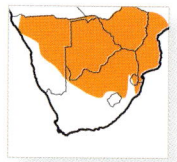
Lilac-breasted Rollers are among the most beautiful bushveld birds of southern Africa. They can be found from Gauteng and Limpopo through to Mpumalanga and in countries to the north of South Africa.

They live in woodland and thornveld, and can often be spotted perched on telephone lines.

As year-round residents, they can be seen most of the year, although they are known to move about, particularly in winter.

 From a perch, they suddenly drop down onto their prey of insects, scorpions, lizards, spiders and even small rodents.

 They nest in holes in trees. Unable to make their own nest holes, they take over those of other birds such as woodpeckers and barbets.

TRACK N° 29

Their call is a harsh, croak-like sound.

30 | Southern Ground-Hornbill
Bromvoël

Adult Southern Ground-Hornbill (left); juvenile (right).

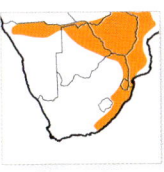

Southern Ground-Hornbills are threatened birds (meaning they could become extinct in the near future) that live only in KwaZulu-Natal, Mpumalanga and parts of the Eastern Cape and Zimbabwe.

Their habitat varies from woodland to thornveld, as long as there are large trees in the vicinity.

They do not move about, staying all year in their particular territory, which they guard from other birds. They have been known to break house or car windows, mistaking their own reflections for competitors in their territory.

 Their diet includes insects, frogs, snails, lizards and snakes; they may even eat larger prey like small rabbits, squirrels and mongooses.

 They make their nest in large holes they find in trees and sometimes even in cracks on cliff faces. Or they may take over abandoned stick nests in the area. They line the nest with leaves and grass. The same nest may be re-used year after year. Unlike other hornbills, the female is not sealed up in her nest while she incubates her eggs, although she does remain in her nest hole for the duration, and is fed by the other members of her group, which usually numbers from 3 to 5 birds.

TRACK N° 30

Their deep, booming call can be heard from far away. From a distance it can sound like a lion roaring.

31 | Green Wood-Hoopoe
Rooibekkakelaar

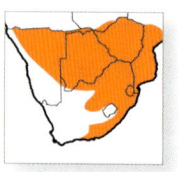

Green Wood-Hoopoes are common in the north-eastern parts of southern Africa, and can be found in KwaZulu-Natal and the Eastern Cape.

They live in woodland, bushveld, at the edges of forests and in well-wooded gardens.

Year-round residents, they almost never move out of their territories.

 Their diet consists mainly of insects.

 They make their nest in holes they find in trees – because they cannot make their own nest hole, they must use those of other birds, such as the barbet or woodpecker, or a natural hole in a tree.

TRACK N° 31

They call in a group – a loud, cackling sound as the birds sway back and forth on a branch, waving their long tails in the air.

32 | African Hoopoe
Hoephoep

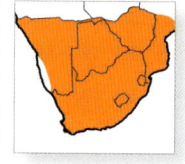

These hoopoes are commonly found in most of southern Africa, except for the dry areas of the Karoo and Kalahari. They can be spotted in woodland, parks or gardens.

In some places they stay put throughout the year, but they are known to move around in others.

 They walk about on the ground looking for insects, and may even dig into the soil using their long bill to get at them.

 African Hoopoes nest in holes they find in trees, perhaps in old nests, or in holes in walls and buildings.

TRACK N° 32

Their call is a very distinctive 'hoop-hoop, hoop-oop-oop', which is where their name comes from.

33 | Black-collared Barbet
Rooikophoutkapper

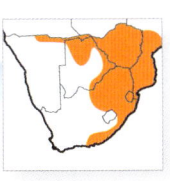

Black-collared Barbets are common residents of Gauteng, Limpopo, Mpumalanga and Zimbabwe. You might also find them in KwaZulu-Natal and parts of Botswana.

They can be found wherever there are fruit trees, but they prefer woodland, some types of forest and gardens.

They never move far from their area, staying in a very small range all year round.

 These barbets love fruit and this makes up a major part of their diet. Put some fruit out and you should see them in your garden.

 They hollow out a nest in a soft tree branch or trunk.

TRACK N° 33

Their unmistakable call is a duet sung by a breeding pair: one bird sings 'too' and its partner responds with 'puddley'. Together, they call 'too-puddley, too-puddley, too-puddley, too-puddley'.

34 | Crested Barbet
Kuifkophoutkapper

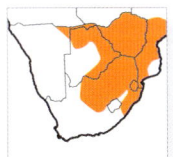

Crested Barbets are found all over Gauteng, Limpopo, Mpumalanga and Zimbabwe. You can look out for these very colourful birds in woodland and thornveld, but they are just as much at home in gardens and parks.

These barbets are resident birds, so you can find them all year round. They do not move very far in their range.

 Their favourite food is fruit, of which they will eat many types. If fruit is not available, they will also eat insects.

 They make a nest by hollowing out a dead tree branch or trunk.

TRACK N° 34

Listen for their call in summer: it sounds rather like a long, drawn-out referee's whistle as they call 'trrrrrrrrrrrrrrrrrrrrrrrrrrrrr'.

35 | Cardinal Woodpecker
Kardinaalspeg

These are among the most common woodpeckers in southern Africa. They can be found almost everywhere except in the drier parts of Namibia and the Northern Cape.

Look out for them in any area with trees, but their favourite home is in thornveld and woodland. You can even look for them in small treed areas within grassland.

They do not move around much, remaining resident in a small area.

 Being woodpeckers, they know how to drill holes into trees, and use their long tongue to get at insects.

 They make their own nesting hole in a dead tree branch or trunk.

TRACK N° **35**

Their call will help you find them – they make a chattering 'tri-tri-tri-tri-tri-tri-tri-tri'.

36 | Rufous-naped Lark
Rooineklewerik

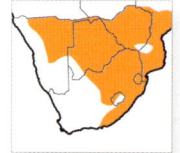

Rufous-naped larks are commonly found from the Free State and Eastern Cape through Gauteng, right up into Botswana and Zimbabwe.

They are most often found in grassland, and some scrubby areas with open patches of sand.

They remain in their territory all year round, and never move very far from their base.

 Their diet is made up mainly of insects, but they also eat grass seeds.

 They make their nest in a tuft of grass, which they pull together to cover the nest like a dome.

TRACK N° **36**

They are very vocal and have many different calls and sounds, mostly a four-noted whistle, 'tri-lee tri-loo'.

37 | Barn Swallow
Europese Swael

These are the most common and plentiful swallows of southern Africa, and can be found almost anywhere.

During the day they fly around gathering food and perching on trees and telephone lines, and at night they roost in reed beds in flocks of up to 3 million birds.

Like most swallows, they migrate in winter and head back to Europe, visiting us in southern Africa from November to March.

 Their diet consists mainly of insects, which they catch as they fly about in the air.

 Because they do not breed in our region, they do not make their nests here.

TRACK N° 37

Their call is made up of many typical swallow-like twittering sounds.

38 | Pied Crow
Witborskraai

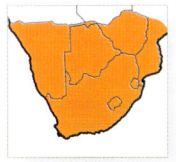

Pied Crows are to be found throughout South Africa, Botswana and Zimbabwe, and also in parts of Namibia.

Their favourite areas to live in are woodland, farmland and shrubland. You can also often find them near where people live.

Because they are resident birds, they can be found at any time of the year.

 Their diet consists mostly of plants, but they also eat reptiles, birds and other small animals. They scavenge, too, and can be found at rubbish dumps.

 They make their nest out of anything from fur to pieces of wire. It is built in a tree or on structures such as windmills and power lines.

TRACK N° 38

They have a typical crow-like call, a 'krraaakk' sound. They also make many other sounds, most of which are quite harsh.

39 | Dark-capped Bulbul
Swartoogtiptol

Dark-capped Bulbuls are common in the eastern parts of southern Africa, such as Gauteng, Limpopo, Mpumalanga and KwaZulu-Natal, up into Zimbabwe.

You will find them wherever there is woodland that has plenty of fruit or berries. For this reason they are also common in our gardens.

Resident all year round, they do not move far and can easily be found, whatever the season.

 Although they do sometimes eat insects, they mainly eat fruit, along with some flowers and seeds.

 Their small nest is made of twigs, roots and grass held together with bits of spider web.

 TRACK N° 39

Their call is a bubbly-sounding 'tip-torop-tip'.

40 | Cape Bulbul
Kaapse Tiptol

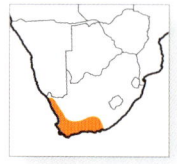

These bulbuls are the southern relatives of the Dark-capped Bulbuls and are found almost only in the Western Cape.

Favourite habitats include fynbos and parts of the Karoo. Gardens are also a popular place for them to visit.

They are resident here and do not move around much, so you can find them at any time of the year.

 Although their diet consists mainly of fruit, they also eat insects.

 They build their nest of twigs, roots, wool and spider webs.

TRACK N° 40

Their call is similar to that of the Dark-capped Bulbul but it is a more grating sound. Listen for a 'dooit-dreet-dooit'.

41 | Cape Robin-Chat
Gewone Janfrederik

Adult Cape Robin-Chat (left); immature (right).

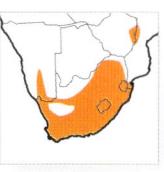 These birds are found across almost all of South Africa, but are uncommon in neighbouring countries to the north.

Even though they like thick vegetation, they also need open spaces for feeding. For this reason, dense woodland and gardens with lots of trees mixed with open areas – allowing them to feed but also get to cover quickly – are ideal for them. You often hear them singing brilliantly in the garden in the early morning or late evening.

They are non-migrants and in some places are resident all year round; in other parts they move between high- and low-lying areas depending on the season.

The Afrikaans name for this bird is Janfrederik, from the sound of its call.

 Their diet includes spiders, insects, small frogs and lizards, along with some seeds and berries.

 The female builds the nest in a hidden spot, such as in a creeper or dense bush. She uses twigs, bits of bark, moss, grass, leaves and other plant material, which she weaves to form a deep cup, lined with soft material such as animal hair or fine plant roots. These birds sometimes re-use old nests, returning to the same site for several years.

TRACK N° 41

These birds have a beautiful, musical song with many different melodies, although each phrase always starts with the same short, whistled note.

42 | Olive Thrush
Olyflyster

Olive Thrushes are common in Mpumalanga and KwaZulu-Natal, extending along the coast down to Cape Town.

Even though they prefer forests, they are frequently found in gardens, where they have adapted well to life in the suburbs.

They are non-migrants and stay in an area all year round so you are just as likely to see them in winter as in summer.

 Being mainly insect eaters, they run around on lawns and in the undergrowth looking for food. They pull insects out of fruit that has fallen to the ground – and may also eat the fruit itself.

 Their nest is a cup made of bits and pieces that they find, from twigs to moss and grass.

TRACK N° 42

These are very musical birds with a pretty song. They sing 'tueeu-treee-dzzudeuu-trrr-preuu'.

43 | African Paradise-Flycatcher
Paradysvlieëvanger

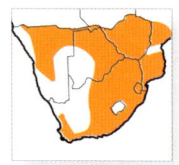
African Paradise-Flycatchers are probably the most beautiful flycatchers in our region and can be found almost everywhere except the Northern Cape and Namibia.

Although they like forests and woodlands, they are also common in many gardens.

They are migrants and generally spend only the summer here, although in certain of the coastal areas, some of them do stay for winter.

 They are called flycatchers because they catch most of their prey of small insects in the air.

 Their nest is a cup made of bark pieces and other plant material, and is held together with spider webs. They often cover their nest with lichen (a type of fungus) to help disguise it.

TRACK N° 43

You can hear their call in gardens in the summer – a harsh, buzzing sound followed by a bubbly, jumbled phrase.

44 | Cape White-eye
Kaapse Glasogie

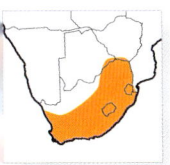

Cape White-eyes are commonly found almost everywhere in South Africa, except in the Northern Cape. They are at home in many habitats and can be found from fynbos to forests, woodlands and thornveld. Gardens are also an excellent place to spot them.

They are resident birds, present all year round.

 They eat mainly insects, which they catch on plants. They also eat fallen fruit and may drink nectar from some flowers.

 Their nest is a small cup of twigs and bark, and is lined with grass, soft plants and even human debris such as hair, wool or string to soften it.

TRACK N° 44

Listen out for their soft calls, one of which sounds like 'peeuuu'. They also make twittering calls to protect their territory.

45 | Cape Wagtail
Gewone Kwikkie

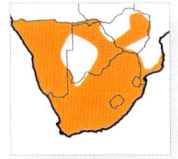

Cape Wagtails are common birds found in almost all of South Africa and north into neighbouring countries.

They can be spotted wherever there is open ground with water nearby, and have also adapted well to living in our gardens.

Mainly resident, they can often be found in the same place all year round, and usually move only if the water supply runs low.

 In the wild they eat insects and tadpoles, but in towns they are known to enjoy the many different kinds of food put out for garden birds.

 Their small nest is made of grass, reeds and other plant material and is usually well hidden on sand banks, in grass tufts or in garden areas.

TRACK N° 45

'Tseep' and 'tsee–eep' calls, together with other twittering sounds, make this bird easy to find by call.

46 | Common Fiscal
Fiskaallaksman

Common Fiscals occur across all of southern Africa, except for Mozambique.

They are easy to find in any habitat, from woodland to open bushveld, particularly wherever there are perches from which to hunt for prey in grassy areas.

These birds are resident, remaining in their small range all year round.

 As predators they will catch anything from large insects to frogs, mice and even other birds if they can. Larger prey is often stuck on a thorn or spike to save it for later on.

 Their nest is made of twigs, bark and soft plant material.

TRACK N° 46

Their call is a rasping 'zeee' sound, mixed in with other harsh, jumbled twittering sounds.

47 | Bokmakierie
Bokmakierie

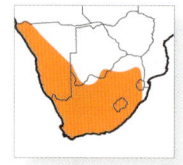

Bokmakieries are common in most of South Africa, except for northern Limpopo. They also extend up into Namibia.

Preferring open habitats, they frequent fynbos areas and grassland where there are scattered perches.

Mainly resident, they can often be found in the same area all year round.

 These predators eat insects, reptiles and even small birds.

 They make a small, cup-shaped nest of twigs and roots, lined with finer plant material.

TRACK N° 47

They have many different calls made up of various trills and piercing whistles. Most songs are duets between couples.

48 | Red-winged Starling
Rooivlerkspreeu

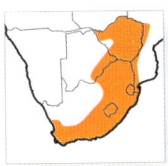

Red-winged Starlings are found in Limpopo, Gauteng, Free State and KwaZulu-Natal, extending all the way down the coast to the Western Cape. They can also be found to the north, in Zimbabwe.

Preferring cliffs and rocky hills, they have also adapted to living in urban areas among tall buildings.

Although they are resident, they do sometimes move to not-too-distant areas in winter.

 Their diet consists mainly of fruit, but they also eat insects.

 Their nest is a flat collection of sticks and is built on rock ledges or on tall buildings.

TRACK N° 48

A variety of whistled sounds make up the starling's call, with 'teeooo' being a common sound.

49 | Common Myna
Indiese Spreeu

Common Mynas are invasive alien birds that were introduced to South Africa from Asia. They currently can be found in Gauteng and KwaZulu-Natal, and are spreading fast.

They are most at home around people, and are often found in large numbers in and around cities, but are spreading into rural areas too.

Being non-migratory birds, they remain resident and do not move about much.

 Their diet is made up of anything from insects to food scraps thrown out by people, and even a wide range of fruit.

 They make a rough nest of twigs and anything useful they can find, even plastic bags.

TRACK N° 49

The myna's call is a collection of many different sounds. The most obvious call to listen for is a 'preeeu trrr-zeeeu trrr-zeeeu'. They are also good at copying other birds' calls.

50 | Cape Sugarbird
Kaapse Suikervoël

Cape Sugarbirds are fairly common, and they are endemic (meaning that they are found exclusively in a particular, limited area) to the Western Cape.

You will find them in their specialised habitat, among the fynbos – and nowhere else.

Being endemic to the area, they do not migrate or move far at all, and can be found in the Western Cape all year round.

 Although they feed mainly on protea nectar, they are also known to eat insects.

 The Cape Sugarbird's nest is made up from a collection of soft plant materials like heather, grass and bracken.

TRACK N° 50

If you listen out for their call in patches of fynbos, you should easily pinpoint these birds. Their 'dzzzreee–zreeeu–dzeu' call is a sound you cannot miss.

51 | Amethyst Sunbird
Swartsuikerbekkie

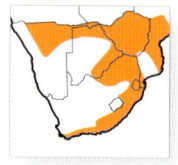

These are common sunbirds of Limpopo, Mpumalanga and KwaZulu-Natal. They can also be found in Zimbabwe.

Their favourite habitat is open woodland and patches of aloes, from which they drink nectar, but they can also be found in gardens.

Even though they are non-migratory, some birds move from one area to another; most, however, can be found all year round in the same area.

 They feed almost only on nectar, but sugar water in garden feeders will also attract them.

 They build their nest of different types of soft plant material, which they tie together with spider webs.

TRACK N° 51

Their call is a single 'teeeuu', but they can also twitter like canaries.

52 | White-bellied Sunbird
Witpenssuikerbekkie

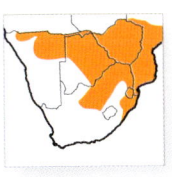

These sunbirds are commonly found in Limpopo, Gauteng and Mpumalanga, extending into Botswana and Zimbabwe as well as Mozambique.

They like woodlands, especially thornveld, but they also visit gardens from time to time.

As non-migrants, they generally remain within the same area all year, but they are known to move around within that area.

 Although nectar from flowers makes up a large part of their diet, they do also eat insects.

 Their nest is made mainly from grass and leaves tied together with spider webs, and they usually build it in a leafy shrub or under a tree so that it has a protective roof over it.

TRACK N° 52

Listen out for their call, which is a 'dzwee tooee' followed by a jumbled twittering.

53 | Southern Double-collared Sunbird
Klein-rooibandsuikerbekkie

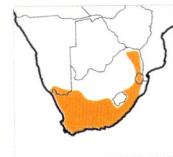

Southern Double-collared Sunbirds are found from the Western Cape and along the coast up into Mpumalanga.

They like many different habitats from fynbos to woodland, forest edges and even gardens.

These resident birds stay in one area all year round, but they can move about within that area when looking for nectar-producing flowers.

 Although nectar constitutes the main part of their diet, they are also known to eat insects.

 They build their oval-shaped nest from soft plant material, tied together with spider webs, and situated in a dense bush or under a tree that serves as a roof.

TRACK N° 53

Their call has a few 'zwee zwee zwee' notes at the beginning, followed by fast twittering.

54 | Cape Sparrow
Gewone Mossie

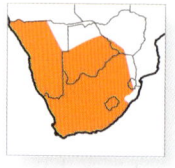

Cape Sparrows are the most common sparrows of our region, occurring in most of South Africa and extending into Namibia.

Their habitat varies from semi-dry areas to gardens and parks.

Because these birds are near-endemic – they are found only in South Africa and Namibia – they never leave these areas and can be found all year round.

 Their diet can be anything from insects to parts of flowers and seeds. They may also eat some fruit.

 Their nest is a large, unshaped ball of grass and other plant material, usually located in trees or on fence posts, or even in roofs.

 TRACK N° 54

Listen out for their typical sparrow call, especially the 'chiree' sound they make.

55 | Southern Grey-headed Sparrow
Gryskopmossie

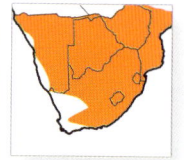

These sparrows occur in most of southern Africa, except for parts of the Western and Northern Cape.

They like to live in woodland and bushveld (wherever there are trees), and even in exotic plantations. Look out for them in your garden, too.

Although they are resident, they will move around in search of food in drier regions. In most areas, however, you will find them all year round.

 They will eat anything from seeds and other plant material to nectar and insects.

 These sparrows make a flat nest of plant material, especially grass, and they may also use softer material like wool.

 TRACK N° 55

Their call is sparrow-like, but the most common sound is a single-noted 'tree-treeu-treeu'.

56 | Southern Masked-Weaver
Swartkeelgeelvink

57 | Southern Red Bishop
Rooivink

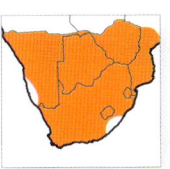
Southern Masked-Weavers are among the most widespread and common weavers of southern Africa. They like places that have trees for nesting. For this reason they can be found in woodland, farmlands and gardens.

They stay in one area all year round. The males have plumage that looks very like that of the females, but they change into bright yellow and black feathers for the breeding season.

 Their diet is made up of insects and seeds, and other plant material.

 They weave a nest like a basket of grass, with an entrance at the bottom; it is tied to an overhanging branch.

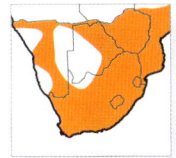
Southern Red Bishops appear in southern Africa wherever wetlands occur.

You will find them in patches of reeds, grassland or on farms, almost anywhere that water can be found regularly.

They are resident all year round, but the brightly coloured males change into a dull brown plumage in winter.

 Their diet is made up almost totally of seeds, but they may eat small numbers of insects too.

 These bishops weave an oval nest with an entrance near the top, and tie it to upright reeds or crop plants.

TRACK N° 56

These birds are easy to find: it's the only weaver to make swizzling 'bzzzzt' and rising 'zrr–zrr–zrr–zrr–zrr' sounds, followed by a dropping 'zweeeeeeeeeee'.

TRACK N° 57

They have swizzling, jumbled calls, but they also make a soft whistling 'srreeee–reeeuu' while they are calling.

58 | Blue Waxbill
Gewone Blousysie

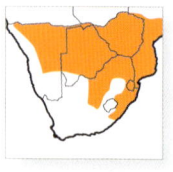
Blue Waxbills are among the prettiest waxbills of our region and are found mainly in Limpopo, Gauteng, North West and Mpumalanga regions, but can also be found in all the countries to the north of South Africa.

They like woodland and bushveld, but are most at home in thornveld.

Even though they are mainly resident, they do move around looking for food.

 Their diet consists almost entirely of seeds, although they are also known to eat termites.

 Their oval, ball-shaped nest is a collection of feathers and soft grass. They usually build it in the outer branches of thorny trees or shrubs.

TRACK N° 58

They are easy to track down, with their piercing 'swee'–sounding call.

59 | Black-throated Canary
Bergkanarie

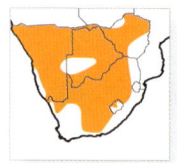
Black-throated Canaries are common and widespread, found in almost all parts of southern Africa.

Their favourite habitats are bushveld and woodland, but they are found wherever woodland and water occur together.

As non-migrants, they remain in southern Africa all year round, and move about only in their own particular area.

 Their diet is made up of both seeds and insects and sometimes nectar is also eaten.

 Their soft nest is an open cup shape, made of grasses tied together with spider webs. It is usually located high up in a leafy tree where it is well hidden.

TRACK N° 59

Like all canaries, they have a very musical call. Also listen out for the sweet, rising call.

60 | Cape Bunting
Rooivlerkstreepkoppie

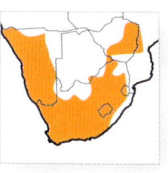

Cape Buntings are commonly found in the Western and Northern Cape, the Free State and into Gauteng, as well as in some of our neighbouring countries.

They spend their time in shrubby patches on rocky slopes and along dry rivers.

These resident birds remain in southern Africa all year round, but in some areas they move about.

 Although they eat mainly seeds, they are also known to eat ants and termites, and sometimes fruit.

 They make a cup-shaped nest of grass, placed either on or very close to the ground, but always well hidden in a leafy shrub.

TRACK N° 60

All buntings have pretty calls, not least the very musical call of Cape Buntings. Listen also for their piercing 'dzeeu-dzeeu-tree-it-tree-dzeeu-dzeeu-tree-dzeeu-treu-treu'.

REFERENCES

Chittenden, Hugh. 2008. *Roberts Bird Guide,* 7th edition. Published by the trustees of the John Voelker Bird Book Fund, Cape Town.

Cornell Lab of Ornithology. 2004. *Handbook of Bird Biology.* Published by the Cornell Laboratory of Ornithology in association with Princeton University Press.

Hockey, PAR; Dean, WRJ & Ryan, PG. 2005. *Roberts Birds of Southern Africa,* 7th edition. Published by the trustees of the John Voelker Bird Book Fund, Cape Town.

Sinclair, Ian; Hockey, Phil & Tarboton, Warwick. 2002. *Sasol Birds of Southern Africa,* 3rd edition. Struik Publishers, Cape Town.

INDEX

Name	PAGE No 	TRACK No	Name	PAGE No	TRACK No 
African Fish-Eagle	10	7	Grey Go-away-bird	17	19
African Hoopoe	24	32	Grey-headed Gull	15	16
African Paradise-Flycatcher	30	43	Hadeda Ibis	9	4
African Penguin	7	1	Helmeted Guineafowl	13	11
Amethyst Sunbird	34	51	Jackal Buzzard	11	8
Barn Swallow	27	37	Kelp Gull	15	15
Black-collared Barbet	25	33	Laughing Dove	16	18
Black-throated Canary	38	59	Lilac-breasted Roller	22	29
Blue Waxbill	38	58	Little Grebe	8	2
Bokmakierie	32	47	Little Swift	20	25
Burchell's Coucal	19	22	Olive Thrush	30	42
Cape Bulbul	28	40	Pearl-spotted Owlet	20	24
Cape Bunting	39	60	Pied Crow	27	38
Cape Robin-Chat	29	41	Pied Kingfisher	21	27
Cape Sparrow	36	54	Red-chested Cuckoo	18	21
Cape Sugarbird	34	50	Red-faced Mousebird	21	26
Cape Turtle-Dove	16	17	Red-knobbed Coot	13	12
Cape Wagtail	31	45	Red-winged Starling	33	48
Cape White-eye	31	44	Rufous-naped Lark	26	36
Cardinal Woodpecker	26	35	Southern Double-collared Sunbird	35	53
Common Fiscal	32	46	Southern Grey-headed Sparrow	36	55
Common Myna	33	49	Southern Ground-Hornbill	23	30
Common Ostrich	12	10	Southern Masked-Weaver	37	56
Crested Barbet	25	34	Southern Red Bishop	37	57
Crowned Lapwing	14	13	Spotted Eagle-Owl	19	23
Dark-capped Bulbul	28	39	Spotted Thick-knee	14	14
Diderick Cuckoo	17	20	Swainson's Spurfowl	11	9
Egyptian Goose	9	5	White-bellied Sunbird	35	52
European Bee-eater	22	28	White-breasted Cormorant	8	3
Green Wood-Hoopoe	24	31	Yellow-billed Duck	10	6